The Princess and the Peas

For Bob and Carole, with love ~ C.H.

For Lucy and Harry and the 'Pea-sticks' ~ S.W.

First published 2012 by Nosy Crow Ltd
The Crow's Nest, 10a Lant Street
London SE1 1QR
www.nosycrow.com

ISBN 978 0 85763 108 4

Nosy Crow and associated logos are trademarks
and/or registered trademarks of Nosy Crow Ltd

Text © Caryl Hart 2012
Illustrations © Sarah Warburton 2012

The right of Caryl Hart to be identified as the author
and Sarah Warburton to be identified as the illustrator of this work has been asserted.

A CIP catalogue record for this book is available from the British Library.

Papers used by Nosy Crow are made from wood grown in
sustainable forests.

Printed and bound in China

15 17 19 18 16 14

The Princess and the Peas

Caryl Hart

Sarah Warburton

to the PALACE

no peas!

nosy crow

Lily-Rose May was a sweet little girlie,
Her eyes were bright blue and her hair was so curly.
She lived with her dad in a beautiful wood,
She was kind and polite and was usually good.

She did all her homework and cleaned out her rabbits,
She did not pick her nose or have other bad habits.
She kept her room neat and was eager to please,

UNTIL . . .

... one day, her daddy tried feeding her peas.

When Lily-Rose May found the peas on her plate,
She worked herself into a terrible state.
"But, darling," said Dad, "can't you manage a few?
They're ever so tiny and SO good for you."

Lily ran out – her dinner uneaten –
But Dad was determined
he wouldn't be beaten.

So he went to the library and brought home a book . . .

Then . . .

he pulled on his apron
and started to cook.

the DESPERATE
HOUSEWIFE
How to LOVE
peas
& other
unsavoury
VEGETABLES

He whizzled up peas
into smoothies and shakes . . .

He baked them in biscuits
and put them in cakes . . .

He laid the food out
in a beautiful feast,
Feeling sure Lily-Rose
would eat ONE pea, at least.

But Lily-Rose May said
it made her feel poorly . . .

Her hands were all sweaty.
Her skin felt so crawly.

"My tummy is churning.
Oh, turn the page quick!
I'm going to be terribly,
horribly sick!"

Next morning,

the doctor jumped out of his car . . .

Shouting, "Lily-Rose May, open wide and say 'Ahh!'"

Then he wrote down her symptoms:

> *"Quite pretty, polite,*
> *And allergic to peas."*
>
> He thought he was right.

"With all things considered, I have to assess
This disease has no cure! The girl's a princess."
"You have to be joking!" her father exclaimed.
"She's a princess all right," the doctor explained.

And to prove it, he told them a terrible tale . . .

... Of a beautiful maiden caught up in a gale:

She came to the palace,
all covered in snow,
Crying, "Please let me in.
I'm a princess, you know."

To make sure the poor girl was telling the truth, The queen made a bed piled as high as the roof.

And right at the bottom, she snuck in a pea. Then she tucked the girl in, with a hot mug of tea.

"If the pea wakes her up,
we'll have a Royal Wedding.
No princess can sleep with a
pea in her bedding!"
The poor girl was terribly ill,
all night through.
She did not sleep a wink.
She was bruised black and blue.

You see, every princess
is allergic to peas.
So she said to the queen,
"Do get rid of it, please!"
The queen was so sorry.
She vowed there and then,
To never have peas
in the palace again!

The doctor said, "That is why Lily-Rose May
Should pack up and move to the palace today.
Even ONE pea might kill her. Now, pass me my hat."
Then he wrote out his bill

. . . and was gone.

Just like that.

Lily-Rose May gave her daddy a cuddle.
"Oh, what shall I do? I'm in such a big muddle!
I would so love to live at the palace, it's true,
But I want to stay here, in the forest with you."

"I know," soothed her dad,
"but the doctor knows best."
So they packed all her toys
and her clothes in a chest.

Then off to the palace went Lily-Rose May,
With a promise to write to her dad every day.

The queen said, "How lovely,
a brand new princess!
Here, have lots of jewels and
a pretty new dress.
You'll find all you need
up the stairs in your room,
Just make sure you come down
to dinner at noon."

This isn't so bad,
        Lily thought with a smile.
I could manage to be
        a princess for a while . . .

I've got my own bathroom
        and teddies galore . . .

A whole library of books!
        What girl could want more?

So she put on her dress
and some fabulous shoes,

And had great fun deciding
which earrings to choose.

She placed a tiara
on top of her head.
Then switched on the TV
and bounced on the bed.

The clock on the landing was striking midday,
So she swept down to lunch in a princessy way.
"Ah, there you are, darling," the king and queen smiled.
"You're safe now, don't worry, you poor little child.

We know you've been having a terrible time.
Your own dad gave you **peas**! What a hideous crime.
But now you shall live like a proper princess –
Do you know what we're having for lunch? Can you guess?

Our very best chef made it
'specially for you.
A lovely big bowl full of . . .

"Now, eat up your lunch,

then your training can start . . .

You've got fifty-four speeches
to learn off by heart.

Then there's three hours of waving
to please all your fans . . .

And lessons in smiling,

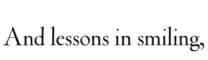

and shaking of hands."

THREE HOURS of waving?
thought Lily-Rose May.

And bowls full of sloppy green
slush every day?

I thought living here would be oodles of fun,
but this is a nightmare! Oh, what have I done?

"I may **not** be a princess,"
said Lily-Rose May.
"And I have to get home
to my dad, right away!

I'm sure I can learn
to eat peas if I try."
Then she gave back the jewels,
and said, "Thank you! Goodbye!"

Now Lily-Rose May is an expert in peas –
She just dips them in ketchup or chocolate or cheese.
Then she gobbles them up, as quick as can be . . .

And she NEVER goes back to the palace for tea.